Presented

By Aunt

.25-42

D1083563

Beyond the Dead-Line in Africa

By

IRMA HEGEL

THE BOOK CONCERN
COLUMBUS, OHIO

BEYOND THE DEAD-LINE
IN AFRICA

CHAPTER I

THROUGH AN ENTRANCE, like the neck of a vinegar cruet, the *Princess Martha* steamed into Kugara harbor. Palm trees stood rooted into the white beach, silent sentinels who looked as if they were guarding the forest depths behind them. A group of naked brown children ran to the water's edge and waved their hands. A house with a queer thatched roof showed itself between the tree trunks.

Fascinated by the strange scenes, Maureen Hammond leaned her elbows on the boat rail, cupped her chin between her palms and watched the moving coastline. All her life she had wanted to see this much-written-about country and now it was before her — a reality!

"Well, Maurie!" Aunt Emma's authoritative voice cut in upon her meditation. Her clear sensible eyes regarded her niece intently. "We're going to land in fifteen minutes. That's what the steward says."

"Yes?" Maureen's voice was dreamy. She continued to watch the exotic scenery: the green trees, the white beach, a red clay road that led back into the leafy interior. "I wonder, Aunty — will Billy be surprised to see us?"

The older woman gave a short dry laugh. "Oh, he'll be surprised all right — I can tell you that much — but he won't be pleased. Certainly the last place in the world for two women is a camp in an African wilderness!"

Maureen smiled. She was a slender girl slightly above average height. Now, as she talked, two dimples appeared in the soft curves of her cheeks; a provoking gleam come into the blue of her eyes.

"You're old-fashioned, Aunt Em! Today women go everywhere that men do; they even do a man's job and succeed at it!"

"Maybe that accounts for the restlessness of this generation," came the sharp retort. "Women aren't content to be women any longer. They want to be men too."

"But they're happy, aren't they?"

"Not in my estimation. I know *you'd* be happier if your father hadn't left you all that money. Look what it's done to you! Put wild notions in your head, brought you here to this uncivilized dangerous country!"

"Don't blame my wanderlust on Dad's money," the young girl responded. "It's something else . . . something here . . . " She put one hand against her heart, held it there a moment. "I want to live life as my brother lives it. I want adventure . . . thrills."

Aunt Emma did not answer. They were going into the harbor then, slowly, cautiously. Whistles tooted. Bells clanged. A pier loomed in view. At the sight, the passengers began to crowd the rail; they pushed and elbowed one another in their excitement.

The older woman stood as unmoved as a statue. She looked down at the incongruous landing before her: the brown-skinned natives, their baskets of fruit balanced on their heads; the important-looking officers in their shiny white uniforms; the naked children who darted back and forth screaming and shouting in a strange shrill tongue.

Maureen was leaning forward. Her cheeks were like pink carnations, her blue eyes, stars. She slipped one hot hand into her relative's. *"Africa,* darling! Isn't it *wonderful?"*

"Wonderful?" echoed Aunt Emma and glanced sidewise at her niece. Of course, the child *would* be attracted to the country! She was only eighteen and youth always sees the glamour of the new and not the danger. When she was forty-nine, things were different then; one looked behind the surface at realities. She thought of what she had read of the tropics; of the lagoons stocked with fever; the rivers filled with crocodiles; the forests where insect pests made travel uncomfortable and hazardous. It was all right when Billy made his decision to go; he was twenty-four then and science and paleology were all in his chosen profession. But Maureen . . .

She glanced again at her niece. The young girl was still gazing enraptured at the pier below them. Her flower-like face was delicately tinted; the wind had caught her brass-colored curls and blown them recklessly about her head. She looked like a lovely dryad.

A girl like this going into the jungle, thought Aunt Emma and shook her head in a savage gesture. "Why did I do it?" she said aloud. "Why did I let you inveigle me into this trip? I must have been mad!"

Maureen looked up and put her arm about the plump waist. "Darling, do stop stewing! You're going to *love* it here! Just see those dear chocolate babies — that big Arab in the turban and djeellaba. It's as if adventure itself were waiting for us!"

"Yes," observed the spinster dryly. "It's waiting all right. And I have a premonition we're going to get more than we ever dreamed about!"

Before she could make herself clear, however, a steward came up to them with the question: "Is your baggage ready?" And the possible hazards of Africa were forgotten in the more exciting reality of landing. A gangplank was lowered; white-coated officers stamped passports and visas; the passengers swarmed ashore.

Caught in the crowd, Maureen and her aunt found themselves pushed into the sweltering confusion of the Customs

Office. Here there was the usual delay, the tiresome questions, the thorough investigation. At last, the ordeal over, they fought their way out into the fresh air, secured a car and rode to their hotel.

In the brief ride, the eighteen-year-old girl caught her first glimpse of an African town. She was a little disappointed. Kugara was not the primitive place she had imagined it to be. There were streets and sidewalks, even American automobiles. Shops and markets lined the thoroughfares through which they passed and a square of white government buildings gave the city an unromantic western appearance.

The hotel, too, was modern in the western sense. It was only when Maureen reached her room and looked down into the grounds below that she recaptured some of her first illusions of the country. She saw, from this vantage point, the hotel garden — a tropical paradise of plants and flowers. There were blossoms of every color: white and purple and flaming red. Among them stalked three magnificent cranes who turned their gold-crested heads from side to side as they moved. A native boy sat near by and strummed upon a gutted instrument wrought in primitive design; a sad song in a minor key.

"Terrible!" said Aunt Emma who was taking off her stiff dark traveling suit and getting ready for her afternoon siesta. "I hope he doesn't keep that up!"

"You're *so* prosaic, Aunty!" Maureen turned regretfully away from the window.

"Well, someone in the family has to keep her common sense and equilibrium. Come — take off your dress and lie down with me on the bed. You'll feel more refreshed for the evening!"

The blue eyes flashed indignantly. "Sleep? My first day in Africa?"

"Silly child! No one runs around in the hot afternoon sun!"

But Maureen clung stubbornly to her decision. "I've got to go out. I want to see the Consul. If we're going to Kivu, we'll need accurate information and advice."

"Wouldn't tomorrow do just as well?"

She bent over and patted Aunt Emma's plump arm. "No, it wouldn't. You go and have your nap, darling! When you wake up, I'll be back with all the data."

"You won't go any farther than the Consul's?" The older woman's face wore a worried look.

She laughed. "No — I promise. Don't you worry now!" Then before her relative could voice any more warnings, she blew a kiss from her fingertips and shut the door gently behind her.

Outside the corridor was quiet, dark. Behind one or two closed doors came the rustle of paper, a snapping of locks; no doubt these were the newly-arrived guests doing their unpacking. Softly she slipped past and went down the stairway to the floor below. In the lobby, a drowsy clerk sat at a desk. Three tourists, two men and a woman who held the inevitable guide-book and camera, were consulting a big map on the wall. A British Tommy stood beside them. He was saying something about the "King's Highway" and the number of miles to Mombasa.

Maureen interrupted his monologue. "I beg your pardon but could you tell me how to reach the American Consul?"

He beamed at her. "Certainly, Miss, certainly! 'E's right across the w'y . . . " waving toward the street. ". . . that white buildin' with the flag on. You cawn't miss it!"

She thanked him, nodded to the tourists and went out into the glaring sunlight. It was hot. The warmth of the morning had given way to the oppressive torridity of tropic noon. The sun blazed down. The heat seemed to shimmer in the air. She crossed the street quickly to escape it. Then, pulses pounding from the effort, she entered the building the soldier had pointed out.

It was a low two-story residence, the entrance guarded by a sleeping porter. She passed him undisturbed and entered a long dark corridor, refreshingly cool after the heat of the street. Here she bumped into another servant, a tall negro in a white tunic, a red sash tied about his waist.

"You wish to see someone?" he questioned.

She nodded. "The American Consul — is he in?"

The servant bowed and threw open a door to his left. "Please enter. . . "

Rather timidly she peeped in. Before her was a dark paneled room lined with bookcases. Several files stood in a row and, at a desk, a young man sat writing industriously. He looked up as she approached and she saw he had sandy eyes, a sandy moustache and a pleasant smile.

"Are you the Consul?" she asked.

He shook his head. "I'm Mr. Weaver's secretary, Joseph Sanborn."

"May I see — Mr. Weaver?"

"Have you an appointment?"

"No-, but my errand is important." She began to talk quickly, eagerly. "You see, I'm William Hammond's sister. I've come all the way from New York to visit my brother at his camp in Kivu. I thought the Consul might advise me as to passports, trains and boats."

The smile vanished from the secretary's face. He looked suddenly sober. "Kivu . . . that's a dangerous journey for a girl alone."

"I'm not alone. My Aunt Emma is with me."

He continued to frown. "It's a dangerous journey," he repeated then added: "Does your brother know you plan to take it?"

"Certainly not! This is to be a surprise!"

"I dare say it will be," said the young man, a trace of sarcasm in his voice. He drummed with his fingers on the desk then shot her a quick searching look. "When did you hear from your brother last?"

She shrugged her shoulders. "It must be four months ago, maybe more. Why do you ask?"

The sandy eyes met hers. "It was just four months ago that the Expedition was abandoned," he said meaningly.

Maureen stared at him. "The expedition . . . *abandoned?* What are you talking about?"

"Surely you can answer that question better than I." His eyebrows lifted in a puzzled fashion. "Your brother must have hinted in his letter . . . "

She came close to his desk. Her fingers gripped the wood so tightly, her knuckles showed white beneath the skin. "Billy said nothing . . . nothing at all. Oh, what is it?" A sob crept into her voice. "What happened up there?"

He patted her tense cold fingers. "Come, Miss Hammond, there's no cause for distress, I assure you. It's simply that the expedition broke up upon Sir Furbish's death. Three of the men came back — Spaulding, Cook and Dawson. They were in rather bad shape: fever, privation — you know the toll the tropics take on white men. The thing that puzzled us, however, was their reluctance to talk. Aside from reporting Sir Furbish's death, they would say nothing. Naturally, the colony gossiped."

"My brother . . . " The two words were all she could manage. Her throat felt dry and parched. "Is he? . . . "

"He remained with the others," answered Joseph Sanborn quietly. "There must be five of them at Kivu."

"You're keeping something from me!" Maureen cried. "Those men who came back — they had to make a report, didn't they? They had to explain Sir Furbish's death?"

"They did that — of course! They claimed he was killed by poisoned arrows. The matter will probably rest there until the others return. You see, Miss Hammond, Kivu is not under the protection of the British. It is beyond what we call the *dead-line*."

Dead-line?"

"Yes, a specified boundary. Travelers are warned to stay well beyond it. And those who venture across must take the fate that awaits them. It isn't healthy country for white men: unfriendly natives, devils, fetishes . . . " He spread his hands in a deprecating gesture. "You understand me now, I hope. You must see why you cannot take the journey."

She looked at him steadily. "But my brother's there . . . . "

He gave her a pitying glance. "Come, Miss Hammond, be sensible! The thing for you to do is wait here until your brother returns."

"I couldn't! I want to see him more than ever now."

He shrugged his shoulders and gathered up some papers on his desk. "I'll ask Mr. Weaver if he'll see you. If I've failed to convince you, perhaps he can."

CHAPTER II

THE CONSUL was a fatherly man with silver-white hair and kindly eyes. He addressed Maureen in a gentle voice: "Mr. Sanborn has told me you wish to go to Kivu. Is that right?"

"Yes!" Her answer was firm, unafraid.

"But my dear young lady . . . "

"If *your* brother were there," she interrupted. "Wouldn't *you* go, Mr. Weaver?"

He gave her a puzzled smile. "That's hardly a fair question. I'm a man, remember, you are not. The jungle, I might add, is hardly the place for any of your sex. I think it would be a much better plan if you and your aunt remained here and awaited your brother's return."

"Wait!" she echoed and glared at the dignified old gentleman who was so secure in his judgment, so wholly concerned with feminine safety. "Do you suppose I could sit contentedly here while somewhere out in that wilderness my brother is in danger . . . "

"Wouldn't your presence add to his danger?" asked Mr. Weaver in the same patient voice.

"But I must know," she insisted. "Suppose he isn't in the camp at Kivu. Suppose . . . "

"Dear child, what we imagine and what truly exists are two different factors."

That made her angry. "I'm determined to go!" she said sharply.

He sighed and leaned back in his chair. "I can give you a pass only as far as Jibouti. At that point you are out of British jurisdiction."

She was as calm and self-composed as he was. "Of course, there is a train to Jibouti?"

He elevated his eyebrows and made a gesture of impatience. "Yes, there is a train to Jibouti. From that town, you must proceed by river-boat." He stared at her curiously. "Have you ever been on an African river-boat?"

"I'm not afraid!" she answered, determined that he would not frighten her off. "I want to see my brother and I don't care what way or how I get to him."

"All right!" The Consul was turning to some papers on his desk. "I'll do what I can to help you. But understand — you are going without my sanction or the protection of your government. You're traveling at your own risk!" Then, as she nodded her approval, he launched into a concise discussion of the route, the guides, the varied stop-overs.

An hour later, when Maureen left his office, she had her passport approved, the initial portion of her journey mapped out and much of the red-tape attendant to travel in Africa carefully abbreviated.

Once more she walked across the street, still glaring but not quite as hot. It was then about half past four. People had begun to appear on the walks and verandas. A rickshaw creaked down the narrow thoroughfare; it was a queer-looking conveyance with egg-shaped wheels. In it sat the perspiring woman tourist who had been in the hotel lobby. Her camera and guide-book were still clutched in her hand; her face was the color of a ripe tomato. Between the shafts of the rickshaw panted a straining native. She must have been a heavy load to pull!

Maureen smiled yet felt a twinge of envy. "There'll be no sightseeing for us," she decided moodily. "If we can get tickets tonight, we'll probably start off early tomorrow morning. But first I've got to do the hard thing — convince Aunty!"

She reached the hotel and found her relative in the room, completely dressed, eager to hear the news.

Maureen was as eager to tell it. She pulled off her hat and flung herself beside the older woman on the broad settee. Word for word, she repeated the entire story; both the interview with Joseph Sanborn and the talk with the Consul.

Aunt Emma did not interrupt. She listened, her plump face grave, her eyes intent on the flushed young face beside her. It was only when the story was over, that she gave vent to her feelings.

"I don't like it!" she said in her blunt manner. "Why did the expedition break up so secretly? Why weren't we notified? And what's the mystery behind Sir Furbish's death?"

"Neither the government nor the Consul will give out any information, Aunty. They say they don't know anything about it."

"Don't know — well, *we'll* find out!"

Maureen's face grew radiant. "You mean you'll go to Kivu? Oh, Aunt Emma, you *are* a darling!"

The spinster made a grimace. "I guess I'm more of an old fool than a darling. But William is my only nephew and, if something has happened out there, I'm not going to sit here with my hands folded. No, I don't like the looks of things — three men returning and the other five remaining. We're going to get to the bottom of this mystery some way."

That night, after dinner, they bought their tickets to Jibouti. At six, the next morning, they were ready to begin their journey.

It was another sweltering day. The sun beat upon the tin roof of the Kugara station and gave the place the atmosphere and smell of an overheated oven. Arabs, in turbans and long robes, sauntered leisurely about. Natives stood in groups, laughing, talking shrilly to each other. White-uniformed officers punched tickets and weighed baggage.

Maureen watched them as they placed her suitcase on the scales and tagged it with a square of bright red cardboard. Then her ticket was punched and she joined her aunt at the crowded entrance.

The train was standing on the tracks; the strangest train she had ever seen. The glass in the windows was blue, eye-protection against the glare of the African sun. The engine burned *wood!*

They were shown into their compartment, a box-like affair with two hard wooden benches. Several minutes passed while they arranged their baggage and made themselves comfortable on the seat. Then the engine gave a shrill falsetto whistle. A guard shouted from the platform. They were off!

Maureen opened the window to get more air. "Besides," she told her aunt, "we don't want to miss any of the African scenery."

As the train thundered through the country, she looked out at the passing scenes. Flat land it was with myriad dome-shaped ant-hills dotting the horizon. Here and there was a smattering of huts huddled together as if for protection. Rocks. Thorny scrubs. Burned brown grass. Occasionally a native came out and stood and stared at the chain of cars that moved so rapidly along the gleaming rails.

Voi was the first stop. It was a small town that boasted only a ramshackle station and a group of sun-bleached buildings. Yet it proved eventful. They were just pulling out when a young man poked his head into their compartment. He wore no hat and his red hair stood up like a russet toothbrush on his head. His eyes were brown and speckled.

"Oh!" he said and blinked at the pair. "Americans?"

Aunt Emma, who was finding the journey rather humdrum, smiled at him. "We're from New York," she announced. "I am Miss Hammond and this is my niece, Maureen Hammond!"

He made a mock bow. "Peter Keyes at your service! A fellow citizen, also a New Yorker." He sat down beside Aunt Emma on the hard seat. "One doesn't often meet American women in Africa. This is pleasant!"

"You know the country, Mr. Keyes?"

"I doubt if anyone really knows it. Is it your first trip, Mrs. Hammond?"

"Miss Hammond!" corrected Aunt Emma who took a stiff pride in her spinsterhood.

"Ah, yes, of course," said the young man hurriedly. "But it *is* your first trip? Good! I may be able to tell you some interesting facts as we go along." He leaned forward and his boyish face grew suddenly enthusiastic. "Tell me, would it thrill you if I said that *Sanseveria,* a valuable fibre grows wild in the bush about here?"

"No! It would bore me!" Aunt Emma said frankly.

"Well, *Sanseveria* is the kind of thing you should know about!" he retorted and turned to Maureen.

She liked him without knowing why. Perhaps it was his homely, good-natured face; his unruly mop of reddish hair, the mischief in his brown twinkly eyes.

Bit by bit, she told him of Billy, his expedition, the mysterious way in which it had been broken up. Peter Keyes made no comment. Only when she had finished, he said in an off-hand way: "It's an interesting trip to Kivu — some splendid botanical specimens there."

She was hurt by his lack of sympathy. "I'm worried about my brother," she said gravely.

He gave her a reassuring smile. "I wouldn't be. No doubt he's safe enough. You ought to reach him in two weeks' trek from Jibouti and I dare say you can get reliable guides at Mimbosa. Maybe I'll join your expedition and help out," he added humorously.

Maureen was going to answer when a cry from Aunt Emma made her turn to the window. There was a herd of wild zebra grazing on a plain. Zebras — *loose!* They looked like an illustration from a child's animal book.

Several miles farther on they saw what Peter Keyes called a *wildbeeste* — it was an animal which resembled both a buffalo and a cow. They talked awhile of African livestock, then the American excused himself and left them. They did not see him again that day.

"A pleasant young man but too much of a fanatic on botany," said Aunt Emma. "I suppose he's a college pro-

fessor or else one of those dull authors who writes about
'Plant Life In Africa' and foolishly expects the public to
read his books."

Maureen smiled and leaned back lazily against her seat.
The heat had grown so intense, even conversation was an
effort.

During the hot afternoon, she managed to sleep awhile.
Then came the magic diversion of the sunset: the coolness
of twilight. For an instant, the country they were passing
through was still, shadowy. Darkness followed with a rush
and low in the heavens a golden slender moon appeared.

Maureen fell under the spell of it. Moonlight in Africa!
The subtle romance — the dreams it wove! How it reminded her of that beautiful Scripture passage, "The heavens declare the glory of God: and the firmament sheweth
His handywork!"

Aunt Emma, however, was growing more and more
disgruntled. Sparks from the engine had burned holes in
her bed-roll and everything else. Her coat, a black alpaca,
looked as if it had the smallpox. All night long she grum-
bled. When she did drop asleep it was to moan and mut-
ter incoherent things about Africa. Maureen, too, was rest-
less and slept but little. She was glad when she saw the
early morning light and knew another day had started.

A glance through the window showed her they were
plowing through the lowlands; the scenery was much the
same as it had been the day before.

At nine o'clock, Peter Keyes paid them a morning call. He had a sticky leaf in his hands which he tried to present to Aunt Emma.

"*The rare Mombasa-verbena!*" he said. "I found it growing by the platform in that last station. Think of it!"

The spinster wrinkled her nose and drew disdainfully away from it. "Why didn't you leave the thing here?" she demanded.

Maureen feared a dispute and came quickly to the rescue. "You must be a botanist, Mr. Keyes. Won't you sit down and tell us of yourself — your work?"

He sat down, the rejected leaf held reverently in his hands. "There's nothing to tell," he said, the twinkle coming back to his speckled eyes. "I was born in New York, twenty-five years ago, educated at Yale; at present, a botanist. There's the whole history in a nutshell."

"You haven't explained what you're doing in Africa," Maureen reminded him.

"Oh, that! . . . " He made a careless fillip. "I've done a little work for the Yale Forestry Department. Finished it a week ago. But I have still two months' leave from the college and I want to stay on — the country fascinates me!"

"There's no accounting for human taste," said Aunt Emma dryly. "Fancy anyone wanting to stay on in Africa!"

Peter shook his head. "If you would only study the *fauna,* the *liana* . . . "

"Well, I won't!" snapped the irate spinster. "Botany is a subject I abhor!"

And that ended the conversation.

Another day went by, another night.

The morning of the third day, Maureen had her first glimpse of real Aborigines. They came to the little hill station, the men wearing a piece of sheeting about their loins, the women clad mostly in brass wire. She would have liked to have looked at them a little longer but the persistent train chugged on. Jibouti was reached that afternoon.

No sooner had they drawn up beside the antiquated station than four yelling natives climbed in through their window and began to struggle for their baggage. Both Maureen and her aunt fought with them to no avail for the natives could understand neither French nor English. Finally one wrested it from the others, grinned and tossed it out of the window to his confederate outside.

Aunt Emma was indignant. Her hat on the top of her pompadour, her coat with the burned holes held about her, she sailed after the miscreants. Luckily, on the platform, they encountered a shabby Arab who wore a brown djeel-laba on which was pinned a great yellow button.

"Our bags!" screamed Aunt Emma.

He calmed her with a wave of his hand. "I am hotel, Misshus . . . I find . . ."

Amid much confusion, much shouting back and forth the missing baggage was finally found and dragged from the unwilling natives. Then Aunt Emma and Maureen, wearied from the exciting encounter, followed the other passengers to the customs shed.

It was a place hotter than the boiler room of a steamer, a scuffling madhouse. Maureen found herself crushed between an enormous mulatto with three evil-smelling pigs in a basket and a naked Somali who kept his elbow pinned against her chest. She tried to move and couldn't. The perspiration dripped from her forehead. Her black crepe dress clung damply to her figure. Then, suddenly, through the dizzy haze of nausea that engulfed her, she heard a familiar voice, a warm hand touched her arm. It was Peter Keyes.

"Like it?" he asked and his speckled eyes laughed down in hers.

"How can you joke?" she groaned. "Why, even the jungle must be paradise compared to this."

"Paradise?" he echoed but he did not finish his sentence. Perhaps he was silenced by the frightened look in her eyes. "You shouldn't have come here," he said quietly. "Didn't anyone warn you, Maureen Hammond?"

CHAPTER III

THE FIRST NIGHT in Jibouti was a hectic one. Most of the passengers from the train had engaged rooms at the Greek Hotel, a flat, two-storied building in the center of the town.

It was a place that smelled of frying fat and dirt but it was the best accommodation the border village afforded. Maureen and her aunt shared a room on the first floor; a foursquare chamber that had a mangy-looking bed (a frayed mosquito netting draped above it) ; a single chair, a rickety washstand. On the door was a flyspecked sign in both French and Arabic, warning guests that everything should be kept under key as the management would not be responsible for any losses.

"A fine state of affairs!" fumed Aunt Emma. "We can consider ourselves lucky if we're not murdered in our sleep!"

When bedtime came, she stoutly refused to undress. Instead, she chose to lie fully clothed upon the bed and made her niece do likewise. For a long time they lay together in the darkness. Sometimes they talked of Billy and made vague predictions; they spoke of New York and home; of the prospective journey through the jungle; of the many events that had transpired in the last few days. Then they would fall into silence and listen to the sounds of the hotel; the splashing of water in a room adjoining; the creak of a bedspring on the floor above; occasional footsteps that moved up and down the hall.

The hours ticked by. Soon there were no more sounds from the rooms about or above them; only the quiet and the darkness.

Maureen was dozing off when she was startled into wakefulness by a long sad moan.

"Oooo! Oooo!" It sounded as if it were right by their window.

She sat upright, dazed, terror-stricken. "A ghost!" she cried.

"Ghost — nothing!" came the brisk voice of Aunt Emma beside her. The spinster was fumbling beneath her pillow. At last, after much scraping and scratching, she drew out her small pearl-handled revolver. She focused it toward the window. "Better not come in — *you,* whoever you are! I . . . I'll shoot!"

"Ooo-ooo-o o o!" came the moaning response.

Maureen waited, one hand to her throat. If *the thing* should come in! But not — it didn't! There was a rustle, a swish and it vanished as suddenly as it had come. Quiet reigned once mere.

"I hope Peter Keyes is safe!" said Maureen in a worried voice.

Her remark irritated Aunt Emma. *"Peter?* Who cares about him? It's your safety and mine that concerns me."

She fell asleep shortly afterward but Maureen couldn't close her eyes. She kept thinking first of her brother then of Peter. Were they safe? Both of them? Odd that she should think of Peter when she thought of Billy and yet . . . . the red-haired botanist had become a real part of her life. She was growing to trust him — to depend on him.

It wasn't until she saw him the next morning that she felt really relieved. They were eating breakfast when he walked into the dining room. He was wearing a baggy suit, his russet hair was as unkempt as ever and his brown eyes had the usual half-dreamy, half-humorous expression.

"Well, Peter Keyes," said Aunt Emma. "Which one of the guests is missing today?"

"Guests . . . missing?" he echoed, a blank look on his face.

"Don't stand there gaping!" she snapped. "You know to what I refer. Last night someone was killed right under our window. I was going to the rescue when the assassin dragged his victim away."

Peter burst out laughing. "I hope you weren't frightened by that moan. I heard it too. It was nothing but a hyena hunting for food among the garbage pails."

"A . . . a *hyena?*"

"Why not? We're close to the edge of things here. Hyenas are as common nighttime prowlers in Jibouti as cats are in New York."

The older woman did not answer him but Maureen noticed that she pushed back her breakfast untasted. Poor Aunty!

So they were *close to the edge of things.* Well, they couldn't be close enough to suit her. Suppose there was danger? What did it matter? Every mile they traveled was bringing them nearer to Billy. In another week she would see him, talk to him, laugh over the experiences they had to reach him.

"Are you going on with us?" she asked Peter.

"Try and stop me!" he answered. Then as Aunt Emma frowned at him, he added: "Plant life in Kivu is very absorbing. I shall enjoy the trip!"

Later, the formality of breakfast over, the three set about getting equipment for their journey. A local outfitter of safaris helped them. He was a plump Frenchman with a black waxy moustache and a shiny bald head. His efficiency was amazing. Before sundown, he had everything arranged. . . supplies, camping equipment, guides. The bill he presented was a long two-page affair and the total (as Aunt Emma ungratefully remarked) looked like the French war debt.

It was too late then to start and they were forced to spend another night in the Greek Hotel. Once more the hyena howled and once more they had a sleepless night of it.

Then, at dawn the next morning, the much-heralded safari to Kivu began. Adeba and Bombo, two porters loaded down like pack mules, led the procession. Aunt Emma, resplendent in sun helmet and tropic kit, followed. Maureen kept by her side. For the occasion she was wearing a white linen suit purchased back in New York; her brass-colored curls were tucked beneath a stout cork helmet.

Behind them walked Peter Keyes, the self-invited guest. He had a "boy" who carried his bedroll and camping equipment but he would not trust to the dusky *wapagazi* a large foursquare case. This, in spite of the heat and its apparent weight, he tugged by himself.

"It contains my botanical instruments," he confided to Aunt Emma.

"I can see how much help he'll be to us!" the angry woman whispered to her niece. "I suppose while we're being chased by wild elephants, he'll be looking at a flower or some silly leaf."

Maureen was silent. Secretly she was thankful for Peter Keyes' uninvited company. He might be absent-minded, a bit too absorbed in botany but he was an American and a white man. In his presence she felt a reasonable degree of safety and contentment.

The party walked the half mile to the river and found the boat. It wasn't a big boat. In some ways it resembled an ancient fishing smack that had seen better days. The pilot was a fierce-looking native who argued long and angrily about the price of transportation, then, the question settled to his satisfaction, he allowed them all to come aboard.

Since there were no chairs, everyone sat down on the deck; the porters in the rear, the three white people near the helm. Their luggage or "kag" as it was now called was piled indiscriminately about them.

A weary wait ensued while the pirate looked for more passengers. None forthcoming, he shoved his boat off and they drifted lazily away; down a broad lagoon with an encircling mangrove swamp, through a creek to the mouth of the river. Now out of the brown water rose a steep hedge of bamboo and palms; they looked as if they were standing on a copper mirror. Flowers of many hues appeared. Birds like gems of scarlet, orange and green, darted in and out among the leaves.

Peter Keyes opened a notebook. Apparently he had forgotten his companions in the array of blossoms and plants before him. He began to write industriously. Aunt Emma closed her eyes and tried to sleep while, at the rear of the boat, the black boys chattered like monkeys, their unintelligible conversation interspersed by frequent titters.

Maureen, for once, enjoyed the solitude thrust upon her and gave herself up to an ecstatic appreciation of the scenery. She was sorry when the peaceful journey was over and the boat docked. The river-port was Abeokuta, a native settlement with only a smattering of grass-thatched *sham-bas*. A night here, then would come the long journey through the jungle to Kivu.

They camped on a sandspit, an uncomfortable spot, for, after sunset, the mosquitoes came in droves and not even the smoke of the campfire would drive them away.

Beneath her mosquito netting, Maureen slept fitfully. A few winks then she would awaken and listen to the eerie sounds of the forest and river. Now a heavy fish would splash, a crocodile would rise and wheeze and plunge again. All sorts of prowlers went about with padded tread. And all the time the campfire burned in the darkness like a great red eye.

In the morning, Peter Keyes, who could speak the language of the nearby natives, secured three hammocks and six more *wapagazi*, porters.

"It's a long safari," he informed his companions. "You will find it's pleasanter to ride than walk."

Many times in the days that followed Maureen had reason to thank him for his foresight. She could never have walked — not those miles and miles through twisted jungle paths; neither could Aunt Emma. Often she doubted if they could have existed without the red-haired botanist.

He was so easy-going and yet so sure. He knew the exact dose of quinine to take, precaution against the deadlly tropic fever. He knew how to mix the boiled muddy water with lime-juice and make it safe to drink. In a crisis, he kept his head even though pandemonium might reign about him.

One never walked surely, that was the insidious thing about this strange, primeval forest. It was undeniably beautiful; the giant trees with their pink and scarlet lichen; the rainbow-colored blossoms; the exotic perfume. Yet there was always the danger lurking behind each leaf and twisted vine.

It was the morning of the fifth day that the safari passed beneath a low-hanging bough. They had been dodging bough-creepers through the entire trip but this time Maureen felt stabbingly painful pricks upon her face and arms. A cry from Aunt Emma and yells from the porters proved they had been similarly afflicted. They were — every last one of them — covered with a writhing mass of tiny worms.

"Leeches!" said Peter calmly. "They attach themselves to your skin and suck your blood."

He called a halt and they spent the best part of an hour in ridding themselves of the vermin.

A few miles farther on an army of ants attacked them. The porters, who were carrying Aunt Emma in her hammock, began slapping legs and ankles and the plump spinster was dumped unceremoniously upon the ground. Fortunately, only her dignity was injured; she was hoisted up again and the safari proceeded on its way.

These were days of adventure; early morning starts when everyone marched and when the black boys sang in a lilting chorus; midday rests where the peace was broken only by the sharp cracking of branches and the gorgeous birds that flitted from bough to bough. Evenings came the dinner, cooked and seasoned like a barbecue; the blazing fire. Then the nights where they slept beneath their netting and heard the barking of hyenas, the deep-breathing of a leopard as it sniffed the fringe of bush surrounding the camp.

On the morning of the tenth day, unexpectedly, they came upon Kivu. It was a settlement smaller than Abeokuta and — disturbing fact — *it was deserted!* No black men rushed out with the greeting *"Jamba! Jamba, Bwana!"* No round-eyed children came to stare at them.

Maureen looked at the empty huts . . . the gaping doorways. "What do you suppose has happened here?" she asked Peter.

The botanist had returned from a cursory examination of the settlement. His flickering brown eyes met hers. "It wasn't a plague or a war," he answered. "To me, it looks as if the native inhabitants had cleared out — in a hurry too."

As he spoke, Abdallah, the head porter, came up to them. The negro's shiny black face was contorted in fright; the whites of his eyes showed plainly. He was pointing a shaky finger toward a dried leaf tacked upon a nearby tree.

"M'wfuti, Bwana . . . M'wfuti!"

"The man looks as if he were going to have a fit," said Aunt Emma. "What on earth ails him?"

Peter laughed. "He says this place has been bewitched. Ridiculous idea, isn't it?" But of course, he doesn't know our Father in heaven." He turned back to the porter, slapped him on the shoulder and gave a brisk command to march on.

The black man turned cringingly away toward his companions. He repeated the command and they filed into line like condemned men; heads lowered, eyes darting furtively to left and right.

"It's the dead-line," thought Maureen. She felt as if an icy hand had reached her heart and was squeezing it very tightly.

Yet, when Peter looked anxiously down at her, she managed to smile back. She wouldn't show the white feather, not while there was a breath of life left in her body. They must be near Billy now! Surely they would reach him!

Into the jungle they pushed, the twelve porters, the three white travelers. It was an uncanny stretch of forest that seemed full of watching eyes. Leaves joined overhead, rank on rank, like a roof of solid green masonry. The air was dank and the earth underfoot gave off an odor of rotting vegetation.

Then, as though the surroundings were not melancholy enough, there came the distant — *bompety, boom, boom, boom* of a drum. Maureen gave a little cry but Peter was quick to reassure her.

"Natives," he said. "Not two miles away. That's an encouraging sign."

"Encouraging?" she whispered. "But if they're un-friendly . . . "

"Or cannibals," added Aunt Emma.

"Well, we'll find out soon enough," he answered smil-ingly. Then, abruptly his expression of amusement changed to one of surprise. "Hello . . . Look! Abdallah's waving his hand. There's a camp ahead . . . *a white man's camp* . . . "

Maureen looked and saw in a clearing, two mud-plas-ter houses with deep-thatched roofs. From the first fluttered a small, faded Union Jack. It was Sir Furbish's expedi-tion . . . *Her brother's camp!*

As Maureen continued to stare at the hut a man came out. He was a big rough-looking fellow clad in ragged trousers and an old torn shirt; a thick stubble of beard cov-ered the lower portion of his beet-red face.

Peter shouted a loud *Hal-lo o o o o!* And the uncouth stranger answered. But Maureen, impatient at any show of formality, darted ahead of the porters, down the tangled path to come to a breathless halt before the *shamba*.

"Billy Hammond," she questioned eagerly. "Is he here?"

The man blinked. He had not expected to see a woman in the party and Maureen, her damp suit clinging to her slender figure, her gold curls tumbling about her face, was a disconcertingly beautiful picture.

"Please . . . " she begged, worried at his silence.

Her plea roused him. "Who are you?" he demanded.

"I'm Maureen Hammond, Billy's sister." An anxious sob crept into her voice. "He *is* here, isn't he?"

The giant shook his head. "No! He's gone like the rest of 'em. There's only me!"

She drew away from him. "Gone?" she echoed, unable to believe the awful word. *"Gone?"*

"Missing," corrected the calm voice of Peter Keyes beside her. "Isn't that what you mean, Mr. . . ."

"Denham. Sam Denham!" came the surly response. "Commissary of the Furbish outfit. Who are you?"

"Peter Keyes."

"What's your business?"

"Botany."

"Botany — *pfaugh!*" The commissary spat out his disgust. "This is a man's country, fellow, no place for you or any of your flower-huntin' fools." He bent down and there was an ugly thrust to his jaw. "Why did you bring this woman to Kivu?"

"There's two women," Peter answered in the same unruffled tone of voice. He nodded in the direction of Aunt Emma now coming flushed and perspiring toward them. "I didn't bring them either. I followed them." He smiled in his good-natured way. "Perhaps if we had something to eat and a little rest, we might explain things all around."

Sam Denham scowled. "All right, come in!" he muttered.

He stood aside and they filed into the *shamba*. It was a man's house, rough and ready with only the plainest facilities for living. No wood was on the floor, no windows in the wall. The air was sour and smelled of stale tobacco and damp clay.

Aunt Emma glanced about her. She had not heard the conversation at the door and she was greatly mystified. "Where's William Hammond?" she asked.

"He's gone!" announced the commissary for the second time. Then in a dreary voice he continued: "Burke and Cadell went first. They marched into that devil's jungle and they never came back. Sir Furbish and Trevor tried it next. They managed to crawl part of the distance here but both of them were wounded. Sir Furbish lived long enough to tell us his story —the weirdest story I ever heard. Dawson, Cook and Spaulding cleared out that same night. They had enough of it."

"And Billy?" questioned Maureen.

"Oh, the tale didn't frighten him. Even with the men gone, he was set on followin' Burke and Cadell into the jungle; me, he made stay and look after Trevor. Two days after he was gone, Trevor succumbed to his wounds and your brother and his two blacks never returned."

"What is this devil's jungle?" asked Aunt Emma in her authoritative voice.

Sam Denham waved his hand toward the door. "It's out there! . . . Five miles of virgin wilderness. Some explorers believe there are caves in it, thousands and thousands of years old. That's what Furbish and his men were after — the exploration of those caves. And Hammond was as obsessed with the idea as were the others. You couldn't hold him. 'Sam,' he says, 'I'm goin' too. You wait for me. I'll be back with Burke and Cadell before the rainy season starts. If I'm not, you follow Spaulding, Cook and Dawson home.' "

Maureen clutched his arm. "And do you mean to say you stayed here and waited without *doing anything?*"

The big man looked at her, his eyes narrowed. "You — what do you know of the jungle and its ways? Think us white folks can do big things, don't you? Sure, we can build railroads, grab the native's country and fight with guns. But I'll tell you something we can't fight — that's black magic. The caves are worshippin' places of the Lalu tribe — they think the gods of their ancestors live inside 'em. Maybe they do because . . . " He lowered his voice to a harsh whisper. *"No one has ever gone near those caves and come back alive."*

Maureen glanced pleadingly at Peter. "But surely we can do *something!*"

"Not tonight," he answered gently. "We'll have a bite to eat and a little rest — that's the main consideration now." He looked at Denham. "You have quarters for the ladies I suppose — that other hut?"

Sam Denham made a grimace. "If they're willin' to risk their necks — of course! I'll have Poli take them over."

Maureen was too sick with disappointment to care for her surroundings. But Aunt Emma, in her usual thorough manner, walked over to the first cot and pulled aside the frayed blanket. Abruptly she stepped back.

"Bedbugs!" she exclaimed. "The cot is alive with them!"

Poli shuffled over to where she stood, curious to know the cause of her excitement. Aunt Emma turned on him.

"Do you know what these things are?" she demanded and pointed down at the bed.

He looked up and showed his white teeth in a smile. "Bugs!" he answered promptly.

"Yes, bugs!" repeated the spinster loudly. "As the house-boy, aren't you ashamed of yourself? You get rid of that vermin right away. Understand?"

He held up his hand. "I fix, Gracious Lady! I fix!"

They heard the patter of his bare feet as he disappeared through the door to the walk outside. Then, in a few minutes, he was back again, a folded leaf in his hand. He bowed and handed it to the older woman.

"No bug hurt Gracious Lady now!" he said and, with another bow, backed toward the door.

For once in her life, Aunt Emma was at a loss for words. She stood there and gingerly unfolded the leaf. And then she received a distinct surprise. The leaf contained nothing but a single kernel of rice.

"My stars and body!" she exclaimed.

Maureen, sad as she was, smiled.

"I don't see the joke," her relative scolded. "What is this thing anyway? Why did he hand it to me?"

"It's a charm, Aunty," she explained. "Long before we came here, I read that the native takes a kernel of rice folded in a leaf to bed with him. He believes that then no bugs will bite him."

"Of all the nonsensical superstitions!" stormed the spinster. "If we're here any length of time, I shall teach that boy American sanitation. He'll find its more result-getting than all his silly charms put together."

Maureen looked away. "Oh, Aunty, how can you fuss about a few bugs when Billy might be . . . " She broke off and covered her face with her hands. Great dry racking sobs shook her slender body.

Aunt Emma laid a comforting hand upon her shoulder. "Now, Maurie, don't go carrying on! That isn't going to get us anywhere. Do you suppose we've come all this distance to lie down and cry and give up? Come, put up your chin, child! Square your shoulders!"

Slowly the crestfallen head with its tangled cluster of curls came up. The swimming blue eyes looked into the spinster's. "You're right, Aunt Em! I — I've acted like a baby but it won't happen again. I'll fight!"

And fight against that gnawing sense of fear she did. That night, when the jungle took on the dark glamour of mystery and shadows danced and crouched about the blazing camp-fire, she dug her nails into her palms and tried to believe her brother was safe, that no harm had befallen him; when half their porters lay down on the ground and refused to work or eat, she told herself tomorrow they would feel differently; they would be ashamed of their cowardice.

Ah, the stark terror of that night! The dismal croak of the frogs; the eternal *tick-tick* of the gecko; the bird that screamed like a tortured human and went plunging down into the shadowy treetops.

It was so hard to stay in the hut and do nothing. Maureen couldn't sleep. She could only lie on her cot and think of Billy. Where was he? What had been the fate of those two men who had braved the menace of the jungle gods? Had he reached them? Were they together?

As she lay there, trying to put the twisted tangle of facts together, she heard the drums again; a slow monotonous rhythm that sounded like a funeral dirge. After a while, there came the chant of many voices singing, then the chorus died away to rise again louder than before.

Aunt Emma rose from her cot. "I can't sleep!" she sputtered. "Between the bugs and that chant!"

"Aunt Em, do you think? . . . "

"Now Maurie, don't let your imagination get the best of you. It's probably some native pow-wow or what ever it is they call their celebrations."

Nevertheless, she came close to her niece and put her arms about her. Together the two women listened. The drums were throbbing in a faster cadence; the singing was growing wilder. As the night advanced, the orgy reached a hysterical climax; the voices died away in shrieks and groans; the drums thundered. Then came a silence so deep, so mysterious, it was as if the jungle itself watched and waited.

"If ever I get back to New York and anyone so much as *mentions* Africa," began Aunt Emma.

At dawn they were still sitting on the cot, their arms tightly fastened about each other, their faces grey with fatigue. The older woman was the first to rouse herself.

"Well!" she said and stretched her aching muscles. "Thank goodness we lived through that night. Let's move around now and get that creepy feeling out of our bones. I'll get washed and dressed first, Maurie, then I'll leave the room to you."

There is a heartening influence in a bath and clean linen. As soon as Aunt Emma left the hut, Maureen washed in the portable basin and changed her clothes. Almost immediately, she felt like a new person. She walked out into the morning sunshine, a crisp look to her fresh blouse, two pink spots like roses blooming in her cheeks.

When she reached the other hut, she found a smell of coffee in the air, the table set for breakfast. Denham sat in a corner and gave her a brief nod by way of greeting. He looked a little cleaner than he had the day before. His red face was freshly shaven and some of the holes in his shirt were sewed up. Peter stood near him, a silent, preoccupied

Peter. Indeed Aunt Emma, who had just bounced in was the only one talkative.

"I've been to your kitchen," she informed Sam Denham. "It certainly looks as if a man had been running things! Do you know that slimy animals with hundreds of legs are swimming about in the drinking water? And that boy, Poli — I caught him trying to strain the coffee through your sock. It wasn't a clean sock either. Why do you permit such laxity?"

"Why do I permit you to stay here?" he counter-questioned. "No one told you to come. No one invited you."

Aunt Emma was shocked by his answer. "You're not exactly courteous, Mr. Denham."

"Courteous, is it?" he said and gave a hollow laugh. "Talking of courtesy when we're standing on the brink of death. Death, old woman, did you hear me?"

The robust matron had never been called an *old woman* before. She glared at Sam Denham but the big man glared just as brazenly back at her. They looked like two roosters before a fight.

Peter watched the pair and decided it was time to intervene. "I thought we were going to have breakfast," he said. "Am I the only one who's hungry?"

As glum as two sulky children the pair came to the table and the four sat down to the meal of boiled rice, coffee and soggy biscuits. Maureen bit into the half-baked bun, took a sip of the watery coffee and then the question uppermost in her mind could no longer be withheld. She turned to Peter.

"We're going on this morning, aren't we?"

The flickering brown eyes met hers. They were unusually sober. "Perhaps it's better to wait a day," he said quietly. "Some of the men deserted us last night. We're a bit handicapped."

Sam Denham began to laugh. "You see, Miss Hammond, your botanist is not the brave man he was yesterday. He has heard the drums of the devil jungle and he understands their warning."

She paid no attention to the jibe. "Peter, we must go on. Let's leave this morning . . . now!"

He shook his russet head. "There are two kinds of courage, Maureen — intelligent courage and fool's courage. Don't let's be guilty of the latter kind. There's too much at stake!"

"But Peter . . . "

"Peter Keyes is right," declared Aunt Emma. "If we can be protected by the delay of a day or two, I'm in favor of that delay."

"Thank you!" said the botanist. He pushed back his plate, got up from his chair and walked toward the door. On the threshold he paused. "I'll be back in a few hours — I'm going to take a look around."

CHAPTER IV

MAUREEN MADE A MOVE to follow Peter but Sam Denham laid a hairy hand upon her arm. "Let him go, Miss Hammond! You stay here. I've got things I want to say to you!"

She stared into his red face and the strange expression in his eyes held her.

"It's the story Sir Furbish told us," he went on. "About the devil's jungle."

"Go on," she said quietly.

"You want to hear it?"

"All of it," she answered.

Sam Denham leaned his arms upon the table. "It's a place possessed of the evil one — this spot. Nary a cross word or an ache did any of us have until we came here. Then things began to happen; fever first, quarrels later — quarrels that split the ranks and started some of 'em talkin' of home."

"You promised to tell me of the devil's jungle," reminded Maureen.

He glared at her. "I'm a-comin' to that. You see, it wasn't until we'd been here a fortnight that the men began seein' the signs of the witch doctor; the crossed palm-leaf, the skull tacked on a tree. It didn't frighten Burke and Cadell; they were positive the caves were in the heart of that *m'wfuti* forest. Wouldn't even wait for the rainy season to end, those two. They started out and they never came back.

"Trevor and Furbish tried it next. The rain had stopped then and the jungle was beautiful — the leaves all green and shiny, the flowers a-startin' to bloom. They had four porters with them and guns and ammunition enough to fight a whole army of bushmen. They weren't afraid neither and so they kept on goin' further and further in. The trees kept thick about them, the underbrush had to be cut with a knife. They began findin' skeletons — a skull here, another there."

Maureen put one hand to her throat. *"Human skulls?"* she whispered.

He nodded. "Aye, they were the bones of men, and Furbish and Trevor should have been warned. Still they kept on. Then suddenly out of a quiet like the grave, out of the green of the trees came the surprise attack. Tiny arrows flew at them from all directions. Before they could protect themselves they were wounded — poisoned."

"Why, of all things!" Aunt Emma exclaimed. "Who attacked them?"

"Who?" croaked Sam Denham in a shaky voice. "That's what they asked themselves. A man can't fight an unseen enemy and —*neither Furbish nor Trevor saw the men who shot those darts.*"

"There are tribes nearby — the ones we heard last night," Maureen suggested. "Do you suppose they . . "

Perhaps?" he echoed. "Who knows?" I've heard of backwoods natives who kill their enemies with poisoned darts blown by the mouth through *sumpitans*. Little darts they are, but the points are dipped in a deadly poison."

Maureen looked worried. "Did you tell Mr. Keyes this story you've told us?" she demanded.

"I told him — yes!" came the ironic retort. "And I might've saved my breath. That fool who sees only leaves and flowers — what does he know of African bushmen or the powers of black magic?" He stopped and brought his fist crashing down against the table. "Fools all three of you! Fools to come here! . . . Fools to stay!"

The blue eyes kindled into two blue flames. "We may be fools, Mr. Denham yet we can do one thing the men of your expedition did not do — *we can stick together!*"

He stared at her. "What do you mean?"

"I'm going after Peter," she said and rose, like a soldier, to her feet. "Come on, Aunt Emma, he can't be far away. We'll catch up with him!"

As she spoke, she seized the older woman by the hand and pulled her through the open doorway.

"But Maurie, are you sure we're doing the right thing?" protested the spinster.

"Oh, Aunty — as if there were any question about it! You go and get what porters we have left together. I know Adeba and Bombo are still with us. They're mission-trained and they're not afraid of any witchcraft. If there are others, get them too. While you're doing that, I'll get our things together and join you at the cook-house."

She did not stop to argue further but ran toward their hut. Once inside, she caught up their sun-helmets, shoved a water canteen and several tins of food into their canvas dunnage bag; piled the medicine kit on top of these, then, the heavy bag slung over one shoulder hastened back to her aunt.

The older woman was standing by the cook house, three porters beside her. These were the only faithful ones.

"Adeba claims he knows the direction Peter took," Aunt Emma informed her niece. "He had his boy, Bukara, with him."

"Let's start then!" ordered Maureen. The fear for Peter's safety made her want to hasten the preparations and speed the departure.

They formed into line, Adeba and Bombo at the head; a fearless porter named Sahar in the rear. Sam Denham stood in the doorway of his hut and watched them.

"You won't come back!" he prophesied.

Maureen merely laughed, waved her head and the quintette started off.

"I can't make you out!" declared Aunt Emma. "Last night, you fairly trembled at the sounds of the jungle. This morning you're going in as brave as a lion."

The blue eyes were strangely solemn. "Peter's in there, Aunty . . . he might be in danger. If he is, I — I'll brave even lions to rescue him."

The spinster started, glanced at her niece. Gradually a knowing smile played 'round her lips. "I understand," she said gently.

The party was entering the forbidden jungle now; a temple overgrown with vines and creepers. Huge chestnut and teak trees stood side by side, their gleaming white trunks bound by creepers with flaming red flowers. Clusters of orchids hung from the forks of the branches. The perfume was heavy, sickeningly sweet; the air was like that of a hothouse, heavy, damp.

Under trees like huge umbrellas they passed; through places where the ground was covered by masses of iridescent fern that changed color like silk. Bright-colored birds darted about and disappeared. Butterflies flew past on gaudy wings.

Maureen hurried behind the porters, blind to the beauty around her. Again and again she asked the same question of Adeba.

"Are you sure we're on the right trail?"

"*Ndio*, Missy — here are branches freshly cut — footprints in the mud."

Still she was worried; still she kept her eyes glued on the impenetrable depths before her. If they would only find him soon . . . if she could only hear his voice again.

She was stepping over a fallen tree when Adeba suddenly held up his hand and grinned. There, not six feet ahead of them, partly screened by the underbrush, was Peter. His botanical instruments were spread about him and he himself was bent above a square board on which was something that looked like a toy canoe. Closer scrutiny revealed it to be a pod; an empty pod.

Aunt Emma's anger could no longer be repressed. Hands on her hips she marched toward the studious young botanist. "Peter Keyes," she said loudly. "Are you studying your botany here?"

He looked up and his homely face had the innocent bewildered expression of a child who is roused from his sleep. "Why Miss Hammond!"

"Yes, it's Miss Hammond, all right!" she snapped. "Aren't you ashamed of yourself, young man? Playing with a silly pod while this girl risks her life and mine to find you?"

Maureen came hastily forward. "Don't scold, please, Aunty! I'm so glad to find Peter safe that what he's doing doesn't matter."

The botanist looked up from the board, his brown eyes radiant. "Were you worried about me, Maureen?"

She nodded and hated herself for blushing. "Terribly worried, but now that we're together again, it's quite all right."

Bukara, Peter's boy, joined the circle then and they all stood round the botanist. The red-haired young man was still staring at the pod. At last he shoved it on the ground, put up his board and began to pack his instruments.

"Do you know," he bagan in a musing tone of voice, "I have a mind to go on and visit those natives we heard last night."

"Have you lost your mind?" exclaimed Aunt Emma. "I should think after hearing that heathenish pow-wow you'd want to stay away, the farther, the better."

"There was nothing formidable in that celebration," he retorted. "If I'm not mistaken it was a *ngoma,* a sort of drinking and feasting holiday they have every time there's a full moon."

"Well, the moon is still full tonight," said the spinster dryly. "If you go over, you'll probably end in a soup-pot."

"Aunty, why don't you let Peter give us his opinion," Maureen interrupted.

He looked at her, his speckled eyes tender. "If you want my opinion, it's this: go back to Denham's quarters with your aunt and let me go on alone. I don't believe there's any real danger now."

She returned his gaze, frankly, unafraid. "I won't go back — you ought to know that, Peter. And certainly if there isn't any danger, we owe it to Billy to go on."

"You're willing to follow my leadership?"

"Haven't we followed it right along?"

He reached over and folded her fingers in a tight, hard grip. "Loyal Maureen!"

Aunt Emma sighed. "No one asks my opinion," she said. "But if my niece goes on, I suppose I must follow."

Peter gave her a grateful smile. "We'll be in the village before sundown, Miss Hammond. But — " He paused, a solemn note in his voice. "There's one precaution we must all observe. You have your waterproof coats with you? Good! Put them on!"

"In this heat?" protested Maureen.

"I'm thinking of those darts that Denham talked about," he retorted. "It was, if you recollect his story, the exposed portions of the men that were the worst infected — the neck, arms, face and knees."

Aunt Emma's face lost most of its florid color. "You don't think we're going to bump into those cannibals, do you, Peter?"

"Suppose we do? We're going to be protected, don't you worry one minute about that!" As he spoke, he drew from his foursquare case, a jar of brownish-colored cream. This he handed to the older woman. "Use it generously on every exposed part of your body," he advised.

She took it with reluctant fingers. "I can't see what good that greasy stuff is going to do me."

"You'll see later on!" he answered and helped her apply the ointment. "Every poison has its antidote you know and this particular cream is the best antiseptic against a peculiar and rare sort of infection."

"How did you know about it?" asked the doubting spinster.

"Through my botanical studies!" said Peter.

"Now you're joking!" she accused him and would ask no more questions.

He seemed oblivious, however, to her skepticism. When he finished with her, he assisted Maureen. Then he gave himself a generous covering and handed the remainder to the porters.

They were a greasy lot when the jar was finally emptied. Everyone looked as if he'd had a mud bath. There was much laughter, a good deal of raillery, then, at last, the party started out.

Adeba beat down the bushes to make a path; Bombo swept vines and creepers to one side while Bukara kept a sharp lookout for prowlers and jungle-enemies.

It was a long march, mile after mile through tangled tropical vegetation. There were no hammocks this time and Maureen could feel the perspiration running beneath her blouse and staining her back. The rubber coat was torture, nothing less. Yet she bore it like a soldier.

Aunt Emma, too, proved herself a good trooper. Not once — though her round face was crimson and she puffed like an engine — did one word of complaint pass her lips.

They marched on steadily, stolidly into the jungle.

It was intolerable effort, endless distance, eternal time. It seemed unendurable this driving oneself forward, keeping to the narrow, tricky path of the jungle.

Suddenly Peter bent down, uttered a sharp exclamation. Maureen turned and saw he was regarding something white. It was a skull — a horrible thing that stared up at them with cavernous eyes and a grinning mouth.

Instantly she was at his side. "Peter, it isn't . . . "

He shook his head. He knew what she was thinking. "No, it isn't a white man," he said soothingly. "This was undoubtedly a native, condemned to death by the witch-doctor."

"I don't understand," she quavered.

He pressed her hand. "It's not a pretty story to tell a girl but since you ask, you might as well know. When a man is found guilty of a crime or misdemeanor, the witch-doctor often mutilates him and then sends him helpless into the jungle to die. If he is sent in without food or water it is just as bad. The prowlers of the night . . . you understand . . . I need not go on . . . "

"No," she said in a hushed voice. "I don't want you to go on — it's so horrible — why I feel as if I were back in the Dark Ages."

"The Dark Ages still exist in many portions of Africa," Peter responded. "And speaking of darkness, look at this place we're in now. I don't believe sunlight has ever penetrated here."

Maureen looked up at the interlaced leaves, the great creepers that wound curtains from tree to tree. The air was dank, the scent of rotting vegetation apparent. It was as if in that dark shadowy thicket, the adverse spirits of the jungle watched and waited.

CHAPTER V

THERE WAS a deadly quiet too; the stillness of furtive watchful things. Maureen had the uncanny sensation that they were being intently observed and followed. Once when a twig snapped in a bush she gave a cry and clutched Peter's hand.

He squeezed it and sang softly in her ear:

> Though devils all the world should fill,
> All watching to devour us,
> We tremble not, we fear no ill,
> They cannot overpower us.

The militant tune and the encouraging words had an elative effect upon her. "Who wrote that, Peter?" she asked.

"Martin Luther. He was a man of courage, Maureen."

"He must have had courage to inspire it in others."

"Have his words inspired you?"

She nodded and followed him more confidently along the torturous path. All sorts of trees now stood thick about them: heavy limes, maples, teaks; the graceful bottle-green bamboos.

A slight breeze came and the bamboo stems creaked and groaned against each other; the foliage quivered. Then, abruptly, Peter's voice, loud and strident, broke the stillness.

"Down on the ground everyone — quick!" To the porters, he repeated the command in Swahili.

Maureen fell where she was standing, hands on the ground, face down. Through the air, all about her, she heard the whistling sound of flying things. Sharp pointed objects flew against her back and arms. The terrible thought assailed her then — they were being attacked by the men of the poisoned arrows.

Peter gave her a gentle push. "Don't be frightened! Go ahead, easy now. Try not to lift your head."

She slid along on her stomach, propelling herself by her hands. A bush caught at her cuff. She paused to release the fabric from the thorn and saw, beneath the branches, a hollow-eyed skull grinning up at her. Ahead, one of the porters gave a howl of pain. He'd been hit!

A wave of nausea swept over her and she closed her eyes. Her head rocked dizzily upon her shoulders. When would those terrible barbarians leap from their hiding place? What would they do to them?

"Go on, Maureen!" Peter's voice again. He was dragging her along, past the horrible skull into a square of clearing.

Now, almost as suddenly as it had begun, the sound of the singing arrows died away; a blessesd quiet hung over the jungle. Weakly the party halted and spread themselves about.

"Are we — quite safe?" asked Aunt Emma in a trembling voice. "Have those cannibals gone?" Shakily she raised herself to a sitting posture.

"We're quite safe," retorted Peter calmly. "You don't have to worry about cannibals, Miss Hammond, because there aren't any around. Our enemy was a plant!"

"A plant?" she echoed in astonishment.

"We studied about it in college," he went on. "I remember the professor remarking that the species was extinct. Certainly our experience proves the contrary."

Maureen heard the news like one in a dream. At last she found strength to sit up and raise her head. She saw Peter was bent above Bombo extricating something sharp and pointed from his shoulder. Weak as she was, she managed to struggle to her feet and reach for the medicine kit she'd stuffed into the dunnage-bag. She drew it out and handed the gauze and cotton to the botanist.

"Good girl!" he approved. "We'll have this fellow fixed up in a minute now."

As he spoke, he pulled a prickly shaft from the shoulder of the man. She saw it was almost half an inch long, pointed at the tip and serrated like the quills of a porcupine.

She watched him wonderingly. "Does a plant have things like that, Peter?"

"The *Agy* has," he answered. "It's a disagreeable poisonous growth that flowers the year round and bears a pod covered with poisonous darts like a needle. These shafts shed in a shower at a touch or even in a breeze. Then the pods refill again.

"Was it these darts that killed Sir Furbish and Trevor?" she asked.

"I haven't the slightest doubt," he replied. "You see, it's as I told your aunt several hours ago, every poison has its antidote. When we studied about this plant in college, our professor, a great student of African poisons, gave us the formula for an *Agy* antidote. I jotted it down and kept it because I was interested in the tropics even then. Later I came here on the forestry expedition and I made up the formula. I was still tremendously curious about the *Agy* and I was bound, if ever I came across one, to be amply protected. Denham's story aroused my suspicions and when I found that pod this morning, I was positive no natives had ever attacked the two Englishmen.

He paused and finished with his patient. "Sir Furbish and Trevor were without the proper safeguard. After they were wounded they used ordinary sterilization methods which were worse than none at all. During the long march back to camp, the poison, unchecked, began its deadly work, gangrene set in and — the rest you know."

She nodded. "If only Billy . . . "

"Your brother, remember, left *after* Sir Furbish and Trevor were wounded," he reminded her. "He knew about those darts and you may be sure that, if he went into this jungle, he was protected. As for Burke and Cadell, they were protected too. Denham, you recall, said they left in the rainy season. If they passed the *Agy* during a downpour, they were in no danger of flying darts."

Maureen was still doubtful. "Then, why haven't they returned?"

He frowned. "I wish I knew! Maybe, in the next village, we'll get some inkling of their whereabouts."

They began to get ready for the march again. Everyone was examined for sticking darts. A few were found in clothing and boots; they were removed, then the party sobered by the terrifying experience, formed into a straggling line. Peter gave the command to start and they trudged off.

The black guides followed the twisting intersecting trail with more caution now; their bare feet seemed to feel the ground. Here they turned to the right, now to the left, ever pressing forward. As they moved on, suddenly, like the beat of a monstrous heart, came the sound of a drum. Several others caught on and the staccatto symphony vibrated through the leafy twilight.

"The village is nearby!" said Peter.

Aunt Emma sighed. "This morning you said it wasn't more than three miles away. I think we've walked four times that distance already."

His homely face looked truly penitent. "I'm sorry, honestly I am, Miss Hammond. It was the singing last night that fooled me. They were near then, the natives, or we wouldn't have heard them."

"Oh, they were near enough," she retorted. "But it wasn't any *ngoma* they were having. It was probably some heathenish rite to this *Agy* thing. I suppose the ignorant fellows think it's a devil-god."

The speckled eyes held a mischievous twinkle. "A good many white people, not heathens, might think the same thing unless, of course, they had the right knowledge about the Creator and His creature things. Botany," he added meaningly, "is a very interesting subject."

This time the twinkle was reflected in the spinster's eyes. "I'm glad you brought that up," she said. She stopped and planted herself directly in his path. Then to the young man's great embarrassment, she lifted his face between her hands and kissed it. "Peter Keyes, next to our heavenly Father, we owe our lives to you. And if I said anything against botanists or botany, I humbly appologize right here and now."

The porters glanced about and began to snicker. Poor Peter! He looked like a little boy who has been caught stealing jam in his mother's pantry. Face crimson, he wriggled from the spinster's grasp.

"It's quite all right, Miss Hammond. You didn't have to apologize, really . . ."

"Well, I did and I'm glad of it!" she said. Then to the porters who were standing still and regarding them amusedly, she raised her voice: "Get on with you — you rude persons! Do you suppose I did this for your benefit?" Hastily, they turned about and marched.

They were passing through a less congested wilderness now. The trees were large but the undergrowth had given way to a slight one through which it was easy to walk by cutting through a bush or vine here and there.

In the distance, the drums kept up their steady beat; *boom, bompety, boom . . . boom, bompety, boom.*

Suddenly Peter halted again and called the Swahili command to the porters.

"What's up now?" demanded Aunt Emma.

"I thought it might be a good plan to signal here," he explained.

"Signal — why? In what way?"

He drew his revolver from his pocket. "I'll fire three shots and see what response they bring. It might be a foolish act and then again, it might be wise."

He aimed straight up in the air and pressed the trigger. Three sharp explosions rang through the stillness. The party stood in line, silent, tense. Not even the porters moved.

Off in the village, the drums had halted their beat. No sound broke the dramatic pause. Then, abruptly, like an echo, came the answering bark of another gun.

Maureen started quite as if she'd been struck by one of the bullets. The natives in the village had no firearms, she was sure of that; and even if they had, they wouldn't signal.

She turned to Peter. "It must be . . . "

"A white man," he finished and smiled. "You know I have an idea our quest will soon be over, Maureen. Whoever answered that signal is coming out for us."

He was right. A few moments later, the three shots came again, nearer. Once more Peter answered with a discharge from his revolver.

Beside him, Maureen had forgotten her weariness, the heat — everything but that white man coming toward them. *If it should be Billy!* . . .

The porters began to hurry, they were eager for the rest and food awaiting them in the village. The whole party moved more swiftly.

Now came another shot — how close it sounded! Then a man's voice, familiar, even at a distance. "Hallooo-o-o-!"

Peter cupped his hands before his mouth. "Halloooo-o-o-o!" he shouted back.

Maureen tried to do the same but couldn't. Emotion choked her. The tears were running down her greasy, salve-stained cheeks, her lips were trembling.

"Oh, Peter, Peter!" she sobbed. "It's Billy . . . I recognize his voice."

She strained her eyes toward the thicket eager for the moment when she would behold that tall lean figure that she loved so well.

"Call him!" suggested the botanist.

She raised her voice. "Billy! Billy Hammond!"

There was no response. It was as if the man in the brush, unable to believe the voice that had called to him, had halted and was waiting.

"Billy!" she shouted again.

This time he must have believed his ears; he knew. She heard the crash of the brush as he surged forward, the gladness in his answering call. "Maureen!"

She ran ahead of the porters, heedless of danger, deaf to warning shouts. Before her in the thicket she saw the tip of a cork helmet — then the underbrush parted — he stood in full view, *her brother!* He was a bit thinner than when she had seen him last, older too. But the sun-burned face, the clefted chin, the reckless eyes were just as they had always been.

"Billy!" She was in his arms, her head pressed against his damp and heaving chest.

He held her very tight. "Maureen, little sister! Thank God, for such a welcome surprise!"

Then Aunt Emma came up, the porters, clustered about them and pandemonium reigned. They couldn't go on. They had to sit down on the first convenient log and talk it over.

Such exclamations! Such questions! Maureen had to tell of the long trip, the hazards, the weary search. Aunt Emma added her frequent opinions of Africa. Then Billy, his arms about them both, told them the story they were longing to hear. He related how dissension had split the ranks of the expedition; of the two geologists determined to find the caves and their subsequent disappearance; of Sir Furbish's death and Trevor's wounds.

"I was positive Burke and Cadell weren't dead," he declared. "Back in my mind, I had the persistent thought that they were prisoners at a nearby village. Of course, Sir Furbish told us about the arrows and I studied his wounds pretty carefully. Where his clothing had been, they hadn't penetrated; the worst infections were in his face, arms and knees; the same with Trevor. I didn't say anything to Denham, he was so convinced it was all black magic, there was no use arguing with him; but, before I started, I made myself and the boy a sort of armor out of canvas. Mighty hot traveling togs they were, yet as long as we got through safely we vowed we didn't mind."

He paused and made a grimace. "Well, we struck the arrows all right and we were grateful for that canvas protection. I fired back just as fast as the darts came but perhaps the attack was simply a warning to keep out of some tabu territory for, when we crawled on, it stopped as suddenly as it had begun."

Maureen interrupted the story at this point to tell about Peter and the *Agy;* then she looked intently at her brother. "I don't understand it clearly yet. As long as you did get through safely, why didn't you return to Mr. Denham and the camp?"

He pinched her ear. "For the best reason in the world, little sister. When I reached the village I found Burke and Cadell had hit upon the greatest paleolic discovery of the age; the Rhodesian caves. Inside these caverns they'd excavated the supposed lost art of Africa; rock pictures dating back to many centuries before Christ. Moreover, the natives were treating the boys fine. They thought because they'd trekked through the devil's jungle unharmed they must be gods. They thought the same of me. Well, the rainy season was coming on and we decided as long as the natives were friendly and weather conditions dry, we'd secure our rock pictures and get them packed. Denham, we knew, was safe. Besides, he'd promised to wait."

"You've cleared up the last of a baffling mystery," said Peter. "I understand everything now."

"I don't understand you," Billy retorted. "Tell me, Keyes, why did you risk your safety and comfort to help two women find a man you'd never seen?"

"Is that such a mystery?" asked Peter. He turned and his eyes, shining and tender, met Maureen's. She returned the glance, proudly, trustingly, the glance every woman gives the man she loves.

Aunt Emma watched them and an indulgent smile spread over her face. She looked at her nephew. "Better give them your blessing, William. I know I give mine gladly. Just so long," she added and shook a warning finger at the lovers, "Just so long as you don't get married in Africa!"